P9-CDH-250

Liverpool

✓ *Chester* 16

a 540
Wrexham 12   *a 529*
a 528   *Whitchurch 20*
Shrewsbury 28   *a 529*

a 442

a 458   *Wellington* 22
   a 442
(76) *Bridgnorth 20*   *Bridgnorth* 14 (72)
   a 442
   Kidderminster 13
   a 422
   Worcester 14
   a 38
   Tewkesbury 15
   a 38
   Gloucester 11
    ‾‾‾‾
    125

For Tommy and Kathleen

PHILOMEL BOOKS
A division of Penguin Young Readers Group.
Published by The Penguin Group.

Penguin Group (USA) Inc., 375 Hudson Street, New York, NY 10014, U.S.A.
Penguin Group (Canada), 90 Eglinton Avenue East, Suite 700, Toronto, Ontario, Canada M4P 2Y3
(a division of Pearson Penguin Canada Inc.). Penguin Books Ltd, 80 Strand, London WC2R 0RL, England.
Penguin Ireland, 25 St. Stephen's Green, Dublin 2, Ireland (a division of Penguin Books Ltd).
Penguin Group (Australia), 250 Camberwell Road, Camberwell, Victoria 3124, Australia
(a division of Pearson Australia Group Pty Ltd). Penguin Books India Pvt Ltd, 11 Community Centre, Panchsheel Park,
New Delhi - 110 017, India. Penguin Group (NZ), Cnr Airborne and Rosedale Roads, Albany, Auckland 1310, New Zealand
(a division of Pearson New Zealand Ltd).
Penguin Books (South Africa) (Pty) Ltd, 24 Sturdee Avenue, Rosebank, Johannesburg 2196, South Africa.
Penguin Books Ltd, Registered Offices: 80 Strand, London WC2R 0RL, England.

Copyright © 2006 by Oliver Jeffers.

All rights reserved.

This book, or parts thereof, may not be reproduced in any form without permission in writing from the publishers.
First American Edition published in 2007 by Philomel Books, a division of Penguin Young Readers Group,
345 Hudson Street, New York, NY 10014. Philomel Books, Reg. U.S. Pat. & Tm. Off. Published in Great Britain in 2006
by HarperCollins Publishers Ltd., London. The scanning, uploading and distribution of this book via the Internet or via any other
means without the permission of the publisher is illegal and punishable by law. Please purchase only authorized electronic editions,
and do not participate in or encourage electronic piracy of copyrighted materials. Your support of the author's rights is
appreciated. The publisher does not have any control over and does not assume any responsibility for author or third-party websites
or their content. Manufactured in China. The art for this book was created with paint, pencil and Letraset on pages from old books
that libraries were getting rid of, the artist found, or people were throwing out.

Library of Congress Cataloging-in-Publication Data

Jeffers, Oliver. The incredible book eating boy / Oliver Jeffers. — 1st American ed. p. cm. Summary:
Henry loves to eat books, until he begins to feel quite ill and decides that maybe he could do something else
with the books he has been devouring. [1. Books—Fiction. 2. Food habits—Fiction.] I. Title.
PZ7.J3643In 2007 [E]—dc22 2006026279 ISBN 978-0-399-24749-1

11
First American Edition

THE INCREDIBLE BOOK eating BOY

by Oliver Jeffers

PHILOMEL BOOKS

Henry

loved BOOKS.

But not like you and I love books, no.

Not quite...

...Henry loved to *EAT* books.

It all began quite by mistake one afternoon when he wasn't paying attention.

He wasn't sure at first, and tried eating a single word, just to test.

Next, he tried a whole sentence and then the whole page.

Yes, Henry definitely liked them. By Wednesday, he had eaten a WHOLE book.

And by the
end of the month
he could eat a whole
book in one go.

Henry loved
eating
all sorts
of books:

Storybooks,

MOBY DICK

dictionaries,

Atlases,

joke books,

books of facts,

even math books.

I love MATH

GAME
THEORY

1.2.3

TRIGONOMETRY

But red ones
were his
favorite.

But here is the best bit:

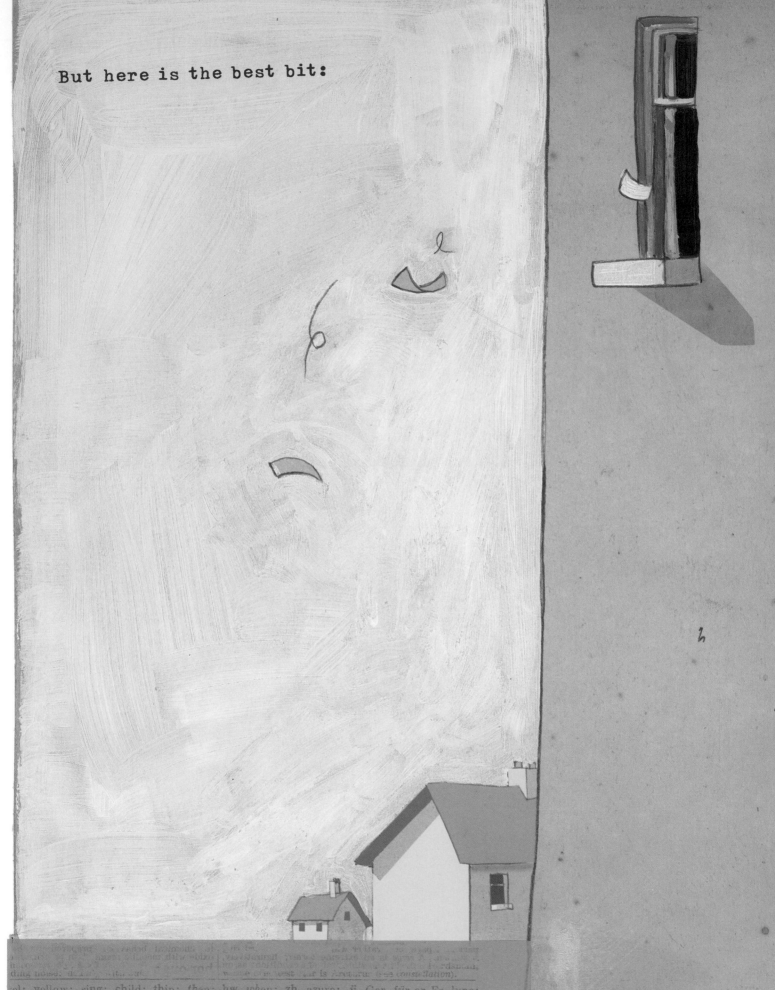

The more he ate, the smarter he got.

A BOOK goes in

B INFORMATION goes to brain [BRAIN getting BIGGER]

C Belly gets FULL

He ate a book
about goldfish
and then he knew
what to feed Ginger.

hmm?

MONUMENTAL

Before long he could do
his father's crossword
in the newspaper,

and was even
smarter than his
teacher in school.

Henry loved being smart.

He thought that if he kept going,

he might even become

the **smartest** person on Earth.

He went from eating books whole
to eating them three or four at a time.
Books about anything.
Henry wasn't fussy,
and he wanted to know it all.

But then things started going not quite so well.

In fact, they started going
very,
very
wrong.
Henry was eating too many books,
and too quickly at that.

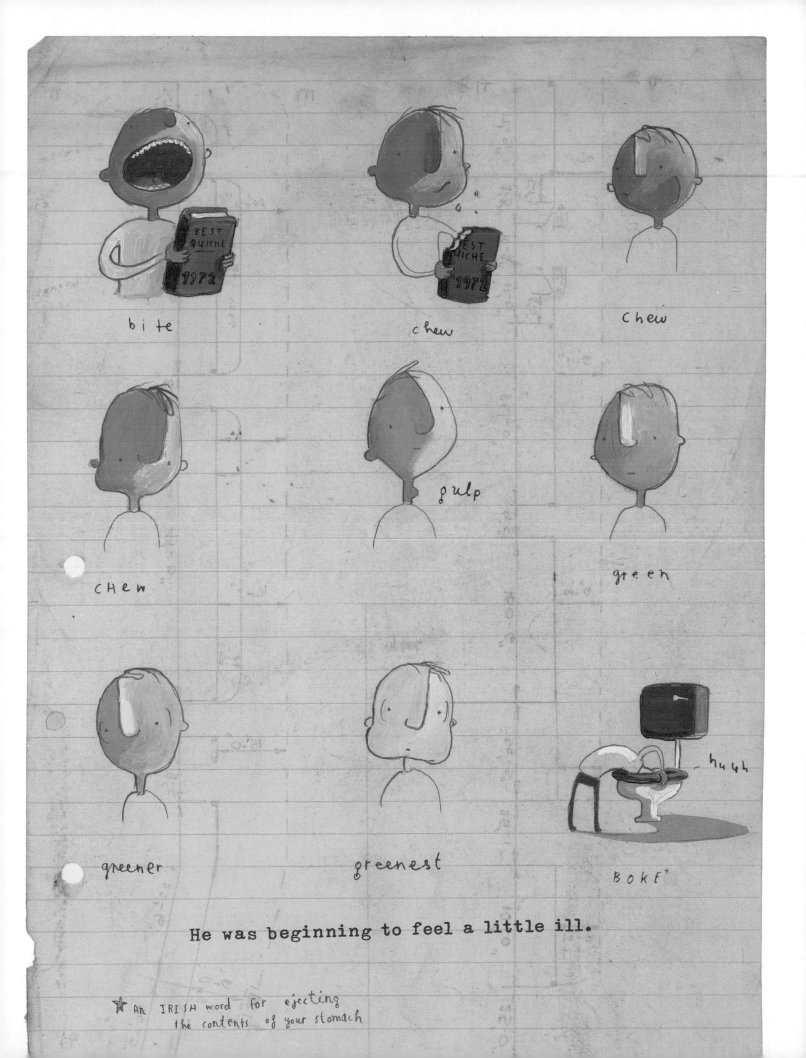

bite

chew

chew

chew

gulp

green

greener

greenest

BOKE*

He was beginning to feel a little ill.

★ AN IRISH word for ejecting
the contents of your stomach

But here is the worst bit.

Everything he was learning

was getting mixed up...

6 + 2 = 3

2 + 6 = elephant

he didn't have time

to digest it properly.

It became quite embarrassing

for him to speak.

20 exemplaires numerotés sur papier de

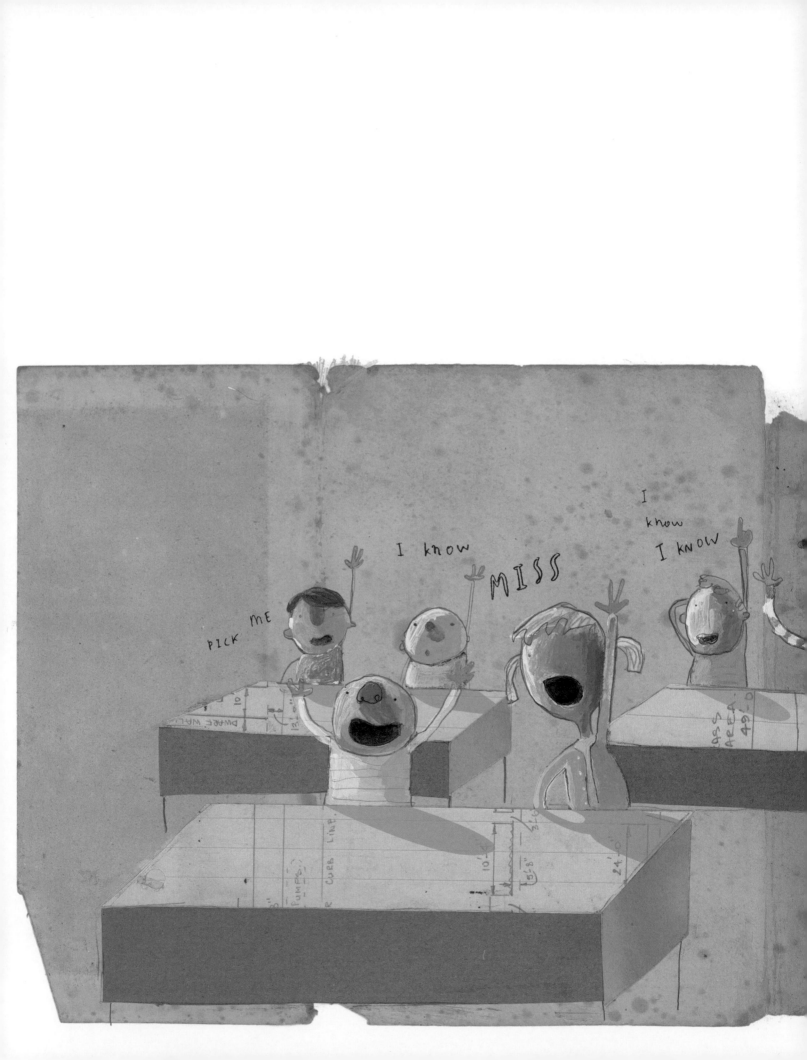

Suddenly Henry didn't
feel very smart at all.

More than one
person told him
he should stop
eating books.

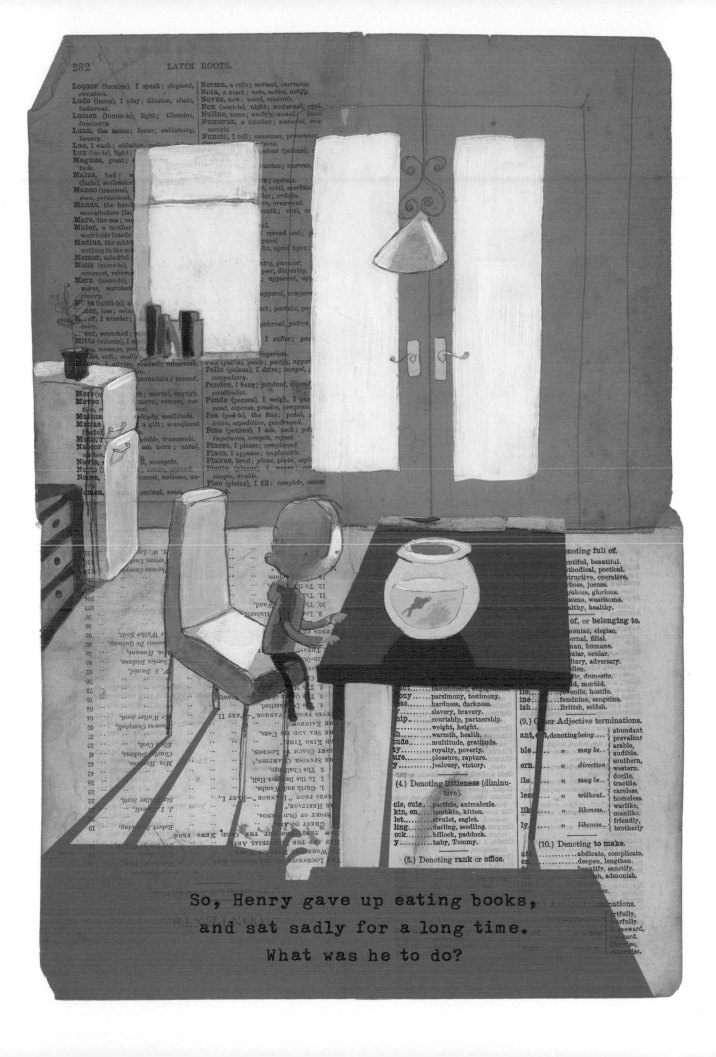

So, Henry gave up eating books,
and sat sadly for a long time.
What was he to do?

Then, after a while, and almost by accident,

Henry picked up a half-eaten book from the floor.

But instead of putting it in his mouth...

Henry
opened
it up...

...and began to read.

And it was **SO** good.

Henry discovered that he loved to read.

And he thought that if he read enough

he might still become

the smartest person on Earth.

It would just take a bit longer.

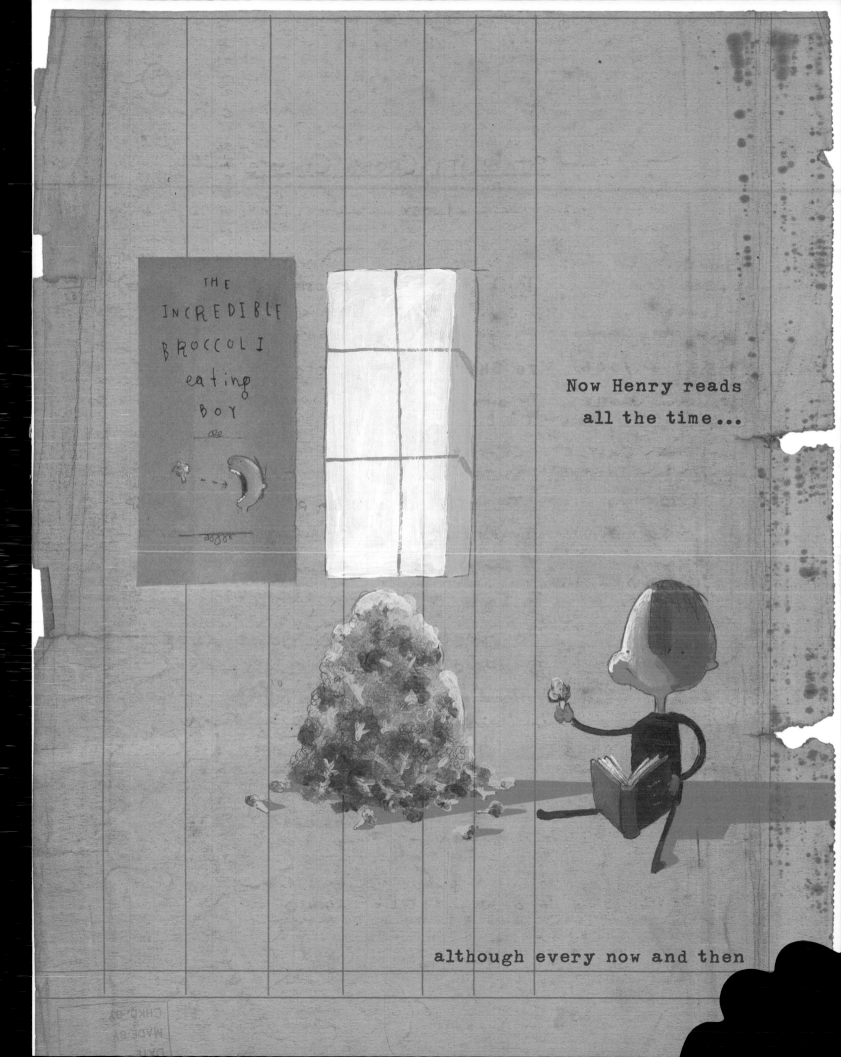

Now Henry reads
all the time...

although every now and then